Tatters from a Royal Yellow Robe

Tales of the King in Yellow
By R. C. Mulhare

Tatters from a Royal Yellow Robe - Tales of the King in Yellow

R.C. Mulhare

Published by R.C. Mulhare, 2023.

TATTERS FROM A ROYAL YELLOW ROBE - TALES OF THE KING IN YELLOW

First edition. August 1, 2023.

Copyright © 2023 R.C. Mulhare.

ISBN: 979-8223229001

Written by R.C. Mulhare.

Also by R.C. Mulhare

Among the Cemetery Trees
The House on Smithen Street, or From Out the Cellar
Tatters from a Royal Yellow Robe - Tales of the King in Yellow

Watch for more at https://www.facebook.com/rcmulhare/.

Table of Contents

Dedicated to the memory of Joe Pulver, the Mayor of Carcosa
1955-April 21, 2020

Publication History

A version of "Paper Masks" appeared in *A Terrible Thing*, Carrion Blue/Atlantean Press, November 2016

A version of "Yellow-Labeled VHS Tape" appeared in *Weirdbook Annual 2: Cthulhu*, Wildside Press, February, 2019

A version of "Yellowvator" appeared in *Deep-Friend Horror* ezine, Deadman's Tome, May 2019

A version of "Grand Staircase to the Yellow Court" appeared in *Secret Stairs*, Silver Empire Press, February, 2018

All other material is original to this volume.

Introduction: Summons from the Court of House Aldonces

Have you seen the Yellow Sign...?

I have no idea where or how I first heard of Robert W. Chambers's *The King in Yellow*, a loose congerie of eerie short stories where the reader never quite feels certain if the things and events which the protagonists describe actually happened to said protagonists, or whether the protagonists have only hallucinated them, after reading an obscure play, allegedly suppressed by government and religious officials, a play that serves as a summoning ritual to open a doorway to an eldritch entity known as the King in Yellow, sometimes identified with the name Hastur. The Chambers stories as well as the fiction which apparently inspired it (two stories by Ambrose Bierce, Edgar A. Poe's "The Masque of the Red Death") later influenced H.P. Lovecraft, that introverted master of weird and eldritch fiction.

I hadn't read any of the King in Yellow stories before the weird summer of 2014, when a dispute between labor and upper management leading to (thankfully short-lived) lay-offs at my day job had me burrowing through my To Be Read Pile, which in turn lead to me picking up The Complete Fiction of HPL. But for the life of me, I couldn't tell you where I had first heard that eerie name. Once I started delving deeper into all things eldritch, I discovered Chambers's work, where that weird name, the King in Yellow, came up. I knew I'd heard this name somewhere, but I couldn't place where. This eventually lead me to the gritty, noirish tales of Joe S Pulver and the first season of HBO's *True Detective*. All this spiraled its way into my psyche, and I found myself, later in the summer of 2015, jotting down ideas for weird tales of my own describing modern day brushes with House Aldonces, of the rise of Carcosa, crumbling kingdoms on the shore of Lake Hali, intimations of dread Hastur lowering over a blasted landscape beneath twin moons and black stars. Several still exist incomplete, but I finished writing "Paper Masks", which I later submitted to an open call from D.J. Tyrer for Atlantea Publishing/Carrion Blue's *A Terrible Thing*.

Three more soon followed, which I have collected into this slim volume (or modest file on your e-reader of choice):

"Yellow Labeled VHS Tape" came to me at an indoor flea market, as I perused a stall of pre-recorded and home-recorded VHS tapes. I amused myself darkly by wondering if a modern day version of a KiY tale would involve an eldritch VHS tape or DVD, much like the one in the Japanese horror film *Ringu* (of which I'd seen the American counterpart). The main character appeared in my imagination full-formed as a composite of aspects from several co-workers (I do in fact moonlight at a local Market Basket), and while writing this, I imagined what could happen if a frustrated young man working retail and trying to find work in a field he'd trained for suffered the full effects of exposure to The Play in any form. The climax of the story came to me during an especially frustrating day at work, when I couldn't help imagining what might happen if a clerk decided to go ape. Part of me worries at how easily this story flowed out of my head and onto the page...

"Yellowvator" unfolded from my thoughts whole cloth, as a Carcosa story, during NecronomiCon 2017 (Providence, RI's every-other-year Lovecraft/Weird Fiction convention, if you've yet to attend), when I wound up using the hotel elevators a lot. I had recently watched some Youtube ritual creepy-pasta videos about the infamous Elevator Game or Elevator Ritual, something I wouldn't even think of trying, especially at a Weird Fiction convention. But I could see someone trying this, hopefully without the results described in this story.

"Grand Staircase to the Yellow Court" grew from an idea lurking in my head for quite some time. I'd wanted to write about a disastrous home theatrical version of The Play, and at the same time, the Internet legend of the Staircase in the Forest had come to haunt me. I got the chance to write a story that put the two elements together when I found a call for stories involving the legendary Staircase. The intrepid Carton Tillinghast, my Carl Kolchak-esque news photographer of the weird who appeared in "The Witch Who Blew In On The Storm", charmed his way into it, capturing glimpses of what had been and what might lurk nearby. The staircase in the story, much like the Staircase of legend, borrowed a good number of details from Madame Sherri's Castle in West Chesterfield, New Hampshire, though I changed the location to a forest two towns away from my home town.

The Yellow King has not finished with me. In due time, I hope to release a companion piece to this collection, a novella which combines the King in Yellow with, of all things, the kind of shop girl romances that Chambers went on to write, leaving weird fiction behind (considering Chambers's cred as a weird fiction author in his day, imagine Stephen King deciding one day to write for Harlequin/Silhouette Romance exclusively). The tale of how that inspiration came to me will have to wait for the introduction to that particular volume. But for now, lock your windows and bolt your doors, and keep an ear open for mad voices on the wind, because His Tattered Majesty awaits a grim audience with you...

R.C. Mulhare
East Manuxet, Massachusetts
July, 2023

Paper Masks

(Carcosa Remix)

"**E**very time I look at this paperwork, I feel like the very words are looking deep into me, scrutinizing me and judging me and finding me lacking," the young client said, watery gray eyes averted from her and from the paperwork that lay on the desktop. To look at her, sitting across the corner of the desk, would mean looking at the papers, fanned out atop the yellow manila envelope.

"I can see that it's hard for you, but it has to be done. You need to fill out these forms to state your case and explain your situation if we're to give you the assistance you need," Cass Archer, the young man's case worker, said, leaning across the corner of the desk, careful not to lean too close, lest he felt crowded.

"I know that in my head, but in my heart..." he paused, rubbing at his stubbled cheek with a still-childlike hand, clearly collecting the thoughts spiraling in his head. "It's like I'm wearing a mask, a mask with a normal face turned outwards for everyone can see and they're fine with it. They suspect nothing, they can't see what I look like and it's just as well that they don't, because if they did, they would see how disordered and damaged I really am. And so... the mask has become my real face.

"But when I apply myself to this paperwork, the mask comes off – tears off, rather – and then everyone, including me, can see my face, how horrible it looks and is," he concluded, his gaze going to the shelves of books against a wall behind her, as if seeking solace in the titles. At least he looked in her direction, if not at her.

"And taking off the mask feels scary and reveals too much," she said, trying to speak his language.

He looked at her that time, nodding slowly, his eyes trying to look hard and confident, for having made that admission, and failing at that expression. He widened his eyes with renewed wariness, rather than narrowing them.

"You know you don't have to fill out all of it at once. Try doing a page or two or a few each day till you've finished it," she said. "You still have time to finish it."

"I'd rather be done with it. I'd rather finish it quickly and be rid of it, be rid of the pain, so I can put my mask back on and leave it on," he said, looking away, He slid the pages back into their yellow envelope before shuffling it into the rucksack he carried.

"Whatever you think will work for you," Cass said, trying to sound soothing, but somehow the words sounded tired and hard even in her own mind. He must have sensed it as well: his shoulders rose toward his ears, as he stood up from his chair to leave. He muttered some standard response about returning as he prepared to scuttle out of the cubicle farm that comprised much of the office space. She rose with him. "I can walk you out, if you like."

"I can handle that much of the path, I think," he murmured, not looking at her, as he took a yellow rain slicker from the coat rack and slipped it on, then scooped up his rucksack as he headed for the hall door.

On returning to her cubicle, she found a book laying on the seat of the chair which the client had occupied a moment before, a book bound in leather, brown turned nearly to black with age and handling, a design like a scorpion or three crooked question marks joined at the point tooled into the cover, tinted with yellow enamel, still vibrant despite the age of the book. He must have left it behind, must have brought with him it to read while he waited to be interviewed. Picking it up, she hurried to the hall door, calling his name, going out onto the landing, looking down the stairs, then going down and out onto the gray and rainy sidewalk, the book clutched close to her to shield it from the mist. Looking up and down the street, past the storefronts and the autumn trees: no sign of him in either direction; he walked fast, that seemed clear. Returning to her cubicle, she slipped the book into a drawer of her desk, to keep it there till he returned for his next appointment.

Before she could close the drawer, Chong, her supervisor, approached, one eyebrow cocked. "Did something come up?"

"No, nothing really, except Castaigne left something behind," she said.

"He's prone to doing things like that," he noted. "I couldn't help overhearing you talking with him: you seem to have set up a good rapport with him."

"He's confused and bewildered by the forms we just sent him, but I think anyone would feel that way: some of those questions can be personal," she said.

"It's good that you established a connection with him, but take care that you don't get too involved in his case: there will be times when you have to ask him the hard questions," Chong said, his tone firm as his gaze.

"But we still have to keep in mind he's a person with a sense of space and the need to guard what's in that space," she said. "When he talked about masks, it made my heart ache a bit. Just for a bit."

"That's quite an image, masks. We've all got masks that we wear when we move out of the safety of our space, but we all need to take them off at some point. Keep reminding yourself that he needs you to help him remove that 'mask' when the time comes," he said. "We need to see what's behind the facades people put up, because we both know people do that to protect themselves sometimes with good reasons, other times not, and that last group includes the fakers trying to get assistance they don't qualify for."

"Oh, there's no question there: I just hate to see him suffer like this: he's such a sensitive soul."

Chong cocked a eyebrow at the open drawer of the desk. "What's that book?"

"He left it behind: I tried to get it back to him, but he'd disappeared by the time I got outside. I'll make sure it gets back to him when he comes back with the paperwork." she said.

"One way he'll ensure he'll return. It doesn't look like the kind of book he'd leave behind without coming back for it," Chong said, with a wry smile, as he moved on to leave her to her work.

More clients, then her lunch break, taken at her desk. She caught herself opening the drawer to peer at the book, lifting the antiquarian covers, scanning its pages, reading some of the text, printed in an elegant, antique font. Its owner had expressed a fondness for poetry and plays, had spoken of writing verse of his own, but she had not imagined that he had such taste, had savored verses as elegant as the lines within.

The book fairly slipped itself into her briefcase and invited itself home with her; something this antique she could not in good conscience leave behind at the office, in case it got lost in the shuffle or shelved where it did not belong. She set it aside, focusing on her evening rituals: making tea, washing vegetables and cutting them up for a salad, but the book intrigued her. Once she had washed up, she took it out of the briefcase intending to flip through it, to see more of what the young man saw in it, to understand what he found in it. Exquisite verses, lush phrasing, no philistine scribbling these, she discovered as she pored over it, till the night sky started to turn pale blue rimmed in yellow. Crash to sleep, to awaken to alarm clock jangling, with just a few hours of rest to sustain her. Fuzzy-headed, staring down at a weight on the duvet, the book fallen open laying there. The book that had come home with her. Come home to her. The book that should go home to its rightful keeper. She got up and made sure that she returned the book to her briefcase, bringing it back to the office, to keep for its keeper, against his return to claim his treasure.

Morning routine, washing up, making coffee, dressing, putting on makeup

(a mask painted onto one's face – where did that thought come from? Oh yes, the book, the masked stranger)

(No mask? No mask!) Couldn't be seen without a mask, or were these masks necessary? So many masks. So many rituals.

Driving to the office, navigating the damp roads, under the misty yellow sunlight. Traffic lights seemed to glow yellow today, she noted, as she dashed through them, running a gauntlet of horns and stares, whizzing past livid visages of consternation and annoyance seen in the windows of other cars.

Viv, receptionist and general office dogs body, gave Cass a concerned puckered frown as the young caseworker entered and signed in. "Did you sleep at all last night?" she asked. "You've got dark circles under your eyes."

(eye holes like a mask)

What? Oh, sorry, no, I didn't: I got wrapped up reading a book. Cassie wanted to admit, but stopped herself.

"I slept just fine," Cass replied, voice even, her tone masking her real intent. So many masks. She hadn't thought, till recently, of how many masks people wear. The client, no, the boy, no, the dispossessed heir, had spoken rightly when he spoke of the mask he wore.

"You sure? You don't have to hide anything from me," Viv said, almost motherly.

"Oh, well, I was up late reading a book," Cass offered, wishing in that moment that she had not admitted this.

"Must have been a really good book," Viv said, as Cass headed for her cubicle.

Fuzzy-headed, thoughts in shreds of rags. *I need more coffee,* she thought, shaking it to cast aside the fuzz, veils that swaddled her thoughts. Veils, masks, visages, more masks, for what she really thought about.

(the whispering of the Tattered King, the wise and kindly Tattered King, the murmuring of the wind across Lake Hali, the sobs of the devotees of the Tattered King as they stagger along the shore under the darkness of the black stars)

No, she only needed her morning coffee, she told herself, as she went for the machine in the staff lounge, make a quick cup, bring it back to her stall in the cubicle farm.

Several cases, some appointed, some drifting in on the cold wind. Yellowing leaves sticking to the windows at the end of the cubicle farm. More clients bearing paperwork, hidden behind masks of names and dates. Conditions and income verification. Doctor's notes and medical records. Numbers and digits. Ciphers and sigils, mere pothooks from which to hang the shreds of ones persona for the vultures to pick clean, leaving the bones of identity. Faces all masks hiding the self within. More masks, her task to peel away. She caught herself wincing, the words of the young man from yesterday came back to her tired mind, cutting more deeply than they did the day before. (the keeper of the book, the masked figure in yellow, no wonder she kept thinking about masks) More scripted verses to chant, to assist the initiates into their places in the mysteries.

No sign of the dispossessed poet. She had not anticipated his return this soon: too many pages for him to fill out (truths to inscribe).

Glances of concern from her clients, looking toward her hands as they spoke and she jotted notes. When one had passed and before the next supplicant arrived, she looked to her papers: in the margins, she had scribbled strange sigils, slow spirals and question marks joined at the point. Where had she seen that? Ah yes, the cover of the book. Why had it gotten under her skin so, had twisted into her mind like a parasite?

(Life/living/existence a parasite that gnaws on everyone of us)

I shouldn't have stayed up so late reading that book, Cass thought, on her fourth cup of coffee in six hours. Why had she done something so unlike her? Ah yes, the poetry of the verses, the strangeness of the tale enacted within, the way the characters became actors in the theatre of her mind.

Office hours ending, and the curtain ringing down on the human comedy (tragedy). She rose from her desk to sign out and head home; Chong stepped into her path as she headed for the door.

"Cass, are you feeling all right? You look pale," he noted.

"I'm fine, I just need to remove my mask..." she stumbled. "I just need some rest: I think I'm coming down with something." (why did she chatter so freely? Wasting words on trifles.)

He took this in silence, his dubious mask a face of concern. "If you don't feel better tomorrow, call me: I'll have someone cover your cases for you."

"Thanks, I just hope I won't need to," she replied. He stepped aside to let her pass.

She found the book still tucked into her briefcase, once she returned home, as if it had secreted itself in there, dogging her every movement. She ordered herself to leave it there as she made herself a cup of chamomile tea

(with yellow flowers)

to calm her nerves. Made herself focus on making the tea: running water from the faucet into the kettle, setting it on the gas ring, taking a mug down from the cupboard, setting it on the draining board, taking down the box,

(yellow box, painting of a figure under a gnarled tree on the shore of a lake...)

(Lake Hali??)

Taking out a teabag, placing it into the mug, taking the just-steaming kettle off the gas ring to fill the mug, letting it steep, taking out the sodden teabag to toss it into the waste bin, sweetening the mug with honey, taking the mug with her into the living room.

To curl up again with the Book, reading it, whispering the lines as the mug of tea on the table at her elbow turned to chilly, yellow-tinged muck, like sand on a lake bottom.

Again, dropping to sleep as the sky turned yellow, though now it edged lowering gray clouds. Dreams this time, of lost Carcosa, twin moons sinking beneath the waves of Lake Hali, black stars glowing dully overhead, fearsome ceremonies in crumbling temples, sacrifices that made one shudder in ecstasy, chants whose melodies twined back on themselves, processions of mute, masked figures winding through the streets of the royal city. The throne of a feuding kingdom soon to be empty, the three heirs to assume it, only one of whom could bear the crown. Through it all, glimpses of a gaunt figure in a tattered yellow robe. A blank white mask of impassivity amidst the grotesque and garish masks of the revelers dancing about it.

Awakening from these strange shadows, quivering with awe. Again, making the mad rush to prepare for work, this day putting on the tatters of the day before and eschewing the mask of makeup. She had to face her clients (subjects). She had to return the book to the young poet (had to see that he gained his rightful inheritance). Running the gauntlet of the streets, lined with autumn trees, dripping with rain and yellowing leaves.

As she entered the hall, Chong looked up at her with concern (mask hiding real intent). "Cass, you look terrible: you should have called me," he said.

"I will be fine: my subjects need me to tend to them," she said.

"Very well, Castaigne called in, said he'd finished the paperwork and he would bring it in today," he said, handing her an appointment list, his gaze dubious.

She felt her chin lift. "Send him to me the moment that he arrives."

The young poet arrived an hour later, the yellow dossier in hand, the formalities to prove his inheritance. He eyed the book laid upon her desk, relief showing behind his mask.

"Oh, you have my book: I thought I'd lost it, when I got home the other day and it wasn't in my rucksack."

"Yes, it has been awaiting you," she said, reaching out to his mask, her fingers stroking the sides warm from the life within. "As I have been awaiting you, Thale."

His mask gathered, puzzled and he pulled back. "What did you just call me?"

"I called you by name. I wanted to tell you that you need not be afraid to remove your mask and show your true face."

"Well, I came here to hand in the paperwork: I finished it yesterday, though it left me feeling like I'd gotten skinned alive."

"That is to be expected, but sacrifice is to be made, to prove that you are worthy of your inheritance, worthy of the crown of Carcosa."

Trepidation contorted his mask. "My what? This is about my benefits: are you feeling all right, Miss Archer?" Proof positive of his worthiness: no worthy heir would rush into this with abandon or grasp at it wantonly, nor without some measure of fear. She would ease him free of that.

"I could not feel more all right, now that you removed my own mask," she said and reaching to him again, set to work removing his.

Gasps from another part of the court, some of the courtiers rushed forward. Her vizier, the usurper with his mask of concern, running to her side, disrupting the ceremony, what must be done to make the rightful heir worthy to stand before the Yellow King. The heir's ecstatic cries, more guards interfering.

The crown would not pass as it must, the masks would remain in place.

Yellow Labeled VHS Tape

(Erase and Rewind Remix)

"Who hauls in all this junk? People that clean out hoarder houses and old people's attics?" Mason grumbled, as he trailed his Aunt Melanie down the main aisle of the Red Dot Flea Market, located in what had been a box factory on the outskirts of Leominister. The place resembled a row of stalls full of junk typical of most attics or basements: one consisted entirely of porcelain dolls, the shelves of another groaned with hardback bestsellers from the last fifty years, including what looked like the complete works of Stephen King. The next one was jammed with boxes of baseball cards, some still sealed in cellophane. Most of the sellers and buyers had put age forty well behind them, except for the babies and second-graders obviously out with Grandma.

"Trust me, Mason, I've found a lot of treasures here,"Aunt Melanie said. "A lot of the sellers don't know what they have on their hands, or they want to move it fast."

"How about they don't move the creepy dolls?" Mason said, looking away from a booth full of kitchen gadgets, FiestaWare and more porcelain dolls. He could just imagine the little darlings with the masks of innocence coming to life and finding creative uses for the orange peelers and egg slicers in the baskets below them.

"Yeah, there's always a lot of those," she said, approaching a large booth of furniture, mostly corner tables, standing desks, an armoire and a heavy carved-wood headboard that lacked a foot board.

"I don't wanna think about why they'd have so many of those," Mason said.

"You wanna keep browsing while I talk with Jake about that armoire?"

"Sure, anything to give those things some space," Mason said, moving on, dodging a woman in a purple sweatshirt and a red church hat with a purple sequined hat band, riding a purple scooter towing a tiny trailer full of shopping bags behind her.

He quick walked past a booth of shoddy-looking tools, and another full of fiber-optic silk flower arrangements and other fiber-optic doodahs.

Wall to wall VHS tapes filled the shelves of the next booth, mostly commercially taped movies and box sets of TV series, some easily available on DVD now and others hard to find, while the lower shelves held bootlegged movies on previously blank cassettes, titles hand-written on labels or the slipcases. In a corner, on the floor, he found a box of tapes shuffled together into a pile. Mason sorted through them, reading the labels: *"The Telephone – Poulenc"*. *"Hopfrog – Poe/DeJasu"*, *"The Driving Lesson"*, *"Titus Andronicus"*, "Ingrid's Monologues and one woman shows", and one with a yellow label with no title written on it.

A shadow fell over him. "You like VHS?" an older man's gruff voice asked.

Mason looked up at a man taller than he, despite how the other's frame had settled from age. "Yeah, I like the format better. DVDs don't have the same quality."

"Too clear, I take it? Yah, something about that picture quality, it's too sharp. And fuggetabout HD or BluRay."

"Even better if it's a home brew tape," Mason said. "The sound, too, it's like that tishy sound on vinyl LPs."

The man looked at him sidelong. "You one of those hipster kids?"

"Not really. I just like old media. What's the deal with this box?"

"Came from some college theatrical troupe. I do clean-outs on old houses, basements, attics. Found this in the back of the living room in an older woman's house, when she was moving into an assisted living facility. Seems the tapes belonged to her niece, was a hippy-beatnik type."

"So the niece was an actress?"

"Yah, told me she kept them after something happened to the niece. Didn't say what. Told me she wanted it to go to someone who'd appreciate them."

"Think I can give them a good home."

"How's twenty bucks for the box sound?"

"Takes me two hours slinging groceries at Market Basket to earn that. How's fifteen sound?"

"Fair price. Thought you'd beat me down to ten."

Mason took out his wallet, counting out three fives into the guy's hand before the guy handed over the box.

Mason met up with Aunt Melanie near the main entrance, where she had the armoire on a flatbed cart, pushing it toward the open doors and the yard beyond where her pickup truck waited.

"Hey, found some treasures?" she asked. "VHS tapes again?"

"Kid, you like some old stuff," said an older guy watching this.

"Yeah, I'll shelve them next to my cuneiform tablets and parchment scrolls," Mason said.

"Got some good movies?" Aunt Mel asked.

"Some kind of home recordings from a hippy theater group," Mason said.

"Didn't think you were into that sort of thing."

"It's fun to watch and snark at the more pretentious stuff," Mason said. "Shake your head over Shakespeare in a laundromat or something like that."

"The heck you got here?" Lexus asked, a few days later when she came to Mason's apartment for pizza and to catch a movie. "God, my grandmother has these."

"Never got rid of the VHS player when DVDs came out," Mason said, hunting up some paper plates.

"So what are these, little kid recital tapes?"

"Some kind of beatnik theater group. Thought we could watch it and have a laugh."

"Really cultured laughing." She pulled up the blank yellow label tape. "This one doesn't have a name."

"Mystery theater. Could be interesting." She handed over the tape. He slid the tape out of its slipcase; the label, also yellow, on the center of the cassette casing read *"The King in the Tattered Cloak – Castaigne"*

"Sounds like a faery tale."

"Or some kinda *Midsummer Night's Dream* thing. How 'bout it?"

"Nothing else, we get a nice bedtime story." He slotted the tape into the machine. The drive clacked and pushed the tape out. "Heh. These things can be stubborn." He pushed the tape back in, firmly, the drive door shutting behind it. The player clicked and clacked as the tape heads engaged and the motors started humming. Mason scooted back to plunk down on the couch, cracking open a soda. Lexus helped herself to a slice of pizza and settled next to him.

The screen lit up, a back-lit off-black square, tracking bars shifting at the top and bottom edges. A single vertical line of static danced down the left hand side. The screen jumped to the image of a hand-drawn and shakily printed program cover bearing the title on the tape label now in neat calligraphy, as vaguely medieval music played. The page slid aside, revealing another card, listing characters and cast members playing them.

"Hah, like those 1940s movies," Mason said. "Like someone's turning the pages in a book."

"I always like those, like you're reading a book and playing the story as a movie in your head."

"It's like they went for that look on purpose. If I didn't want to sound all Film-Student-Who's-Watched-*Citizen-Kane*-Twenty-Times, I'd think it was taped off a TV broadcast."

The play started out as most of these amateur productions did. The costumes looked cobbled together from thrift store finds and bits of fabric in purple and red. The play seemed Shakespearean in scope, if not in language, though it still sounded high-falutin' and literary. It seemed to take place in some made-up kingdom, which they'd given a timeless if vaguely Victorian look, where an aging queen intended to hand over her crown to one of her three children: a kid too young to rule, an elder son too hot-headed to make a half-decent ruler, while the only vaguely competent one, her daughter and eldest child, acted like a dim bulb socialite. Add to this a subplot hinting at some weird cult or the god thereof seducing the elder son.

They'd started on the second act, a scene with a weird old-timey costume party complete with masks (clearly party store domino masks that the costume creators had decked out with whatever feathers and beads and sequins they had on hand). At midnight, the guests would remove their masks. On the moment where the Queen and her daughter confronted an uninvited guest who'd slipped into the party, the screen froze. The tape squealed and the screen went blue. The drive growled and spat the tape out.

"That's odd," Lexus said.

"The hell just happened?" Mason said. "Never had it do that before. Had them shut off and need to be ejected. Had them jam up solid and get stuck, but never making all those noises." He pushed the tape back in, but the drive refused to take it.

"Better than having it get stuck."

He took the tape out and shook it gently before sliding it back in. As before, it would not go in, not far enough to engage the drive heads. "Guess we don't find out tonight which royal kid gets the crown or what the hell Carcosa is."

"What are you going to do with that tape?"

"I know a guy who can fix it. Got me onto VHS in the first place."

Lexus giggled. "Got you onto it. You make it sound like a drug."

"Best legal fix ever."

"Probably dust clogging the mechanism," said Davan, studying the yellow label tape.

"Yeah, but it shuts down and the player spits the tape out. Never had a player do that over dust."

"Could be the tape is twisted inside the case." Davan reached for a screwdriver on his work bench and removed the screws holding the back plate of the tape before removing it. "Hmm..."

"Is that a good 'hmm' or a bad 'hmm'?"

"It's an in between hmm. Tape's not twisted. Probably dust, like I said."

"Like *I* said, the jam wasn't like a dust jam."

"Hand me the canned air. It'll probably clear this up in a jiffy." Mason handed over the spray can sitting on a shelf. Davan shuffled the reels gently to loosen them before spraying them, then put the tape back together before slotting it into the player in a rack of equipment near the work bench. The motors hummed and clicked, but the player stayed still.

"It mocks us," Mason said.

"Like it's tensed up. What did you say this movie was called?"

"*The King in the Tattered Cloak*. Some kind of Shakespeare on meth thing put on by a hippy theater company."

Davan took a step back from the equipment rack. "You serious?"

"Yeah. What's the look for?"

"I thought that was just a made-up story going around on the Internet."

"What, something to scare the kids and the old people?"

"Yeah, it's a creepy-pasta."

"Something involving scary macaroni?"

"No, idiot, it's a story that gets shared around, copy-pasting style, like a campfire story. In this one, you watch the play, you read the play, hell, you act in the play and perform the whole thing before an audience, you go all kinds of cray."

"And you end up dead after seven days."

"No, you go bug-eating crazy for the rest of your life, saying some tatty king or something else is coming for you."

"Right, campfire story like the guy with the hook for a hand who scratches up your car or hooks you dead if he catches you on lovers' lane."

"Which had it's own grounding in reality. Ever watch that documentary *Killer Legends*? Turns out there really was a guy out killing couples in cars, back in the 1940s or something."

"Weird. But back to the tape."

"If it's locking up, and if this tape is what I think it is, you could be getting lucky and something's protecting your pasty butt."

"Protecting me from what?"

"Whatever it is about the play that makes people go bat crap cray and cut other people. I ain't tinkering with this tape one more minute. I say you dodged a bullet and you leave it be. I don't want you going bonkers and literally chewing Lexus's face. Or your own. I don't want that on my conscience."

"You sound like those crazies that think violent video games make people turn into crazy killers."

"I'm only telling you what I heard."

"If I get any crazy ideas, I'll check into the hospital. Try backing the tape up."

"All right, but here's the part where the genre-savvy friend tells the over-confident protag, 'Don't say I didn't warn you'. Do I want to know what you're looking for?"

"Just want to see if the tape loosened up."

Davan threw him a Look, put on a pair of noise-canceling headphones not plugged into anything, then slid the tape back into the machine, rewound it and averted his eyes from the screen as he hit 'play'.

Mason watched the screen, now showing the masked ball scene, the queen confronting the uninvited guest. Behind him, a figure loomed up, which Mason didn't recall seeing during his first viewing.

"Oh crap," Mason said.

Davan hit the pause button. "What? Do I dare look at the screen?"

"I think I saw something in the background that wasn't there before."

"Too much information."

"Maybe I just missed it the first time."

"Maybe it's whatever makes people go crazy when they've watched the thing."

"Or it could be something in the background that looked like a figure."

Davan stopped the tape and ejected it, holding it at arm's length. "If you said it wasn't there before, it probably wasn't there before. I'd nope out of this movie, if I were you."

Mason took the tape. "Good thing I'm not you."

That night, Mason had a shift at the grocery store, rounding up stray shopping carriages under the circles of yellow light cast by the sodium lamps in the parking lot. "You all right out there?" Martin, the front end manager, asked. "You've been out there a while."

"Busy day, lots of stray carts," Mason said. "Don't send the search party for me just yet."

Once home after his shift, Mason called Lexus to ask her if she wanted to come over and watch the rest of the play.

The line went quiet for a moment, aside from some line noise pulsing, like a staticked heartbeat or a distant drum. "I'm not sure I want to watch the rest of that tape with you."

"Why, you too busy with schoolwork or something?"

"That's part of it. I've got a paper due. The rest is... well, it's going to take some explaining."

"All right, let's hear it." He couldn't help wondering if she merely wanted to stall him.

"I dug around, looking for information on that theater troupe that put on the play."

"And?"

"Have you watched the rest of the tape?"

"No. Why?" he lied.

"There's a scene that's pretty gory. Eye-gouging and skin-clawing and face-peeling, like something out of a really gruesome torture-porn movie."

"Straight up Eli Roth, eh?"

"Yeah. Except, it... wasn't stage blood and prosthetics."

"Like a snuff film? You know those aren't as common as people think."

"Well, this is one of the rare real ones. It sounded crazy to me, so I talked to Sheilagh Stamos about it. Her dad has access to a lot of law enforcement data bases, so I asked her if she could ask him to take a look."

"Isn't that illegal?"

"No, and he was glad to help. He's one of the chill people in the FBI."

"So what happened?"

"It happened about thirty years ago, when they still used VHS a lot. Some post-college age hippy-types put together their own theater troupe."

He glanced at the box of tapes, sitting on the coffee table. "Anyone named Ingrid involved?"

"Ingrid Blaxton. I think she played Camilla in the play. She survived, but she's been in and out of mental hospitals, and she needed a lot of plastic surgery. She still insists that a King in a pale mask awaits her in another world."

"Must've smoked some extra hard version of the Devil's Lettuce or whatever they were on in the Eighties."

"That's just it: the kids got tested when they first got brought to the hospital, but they came up clean."

"Unless they got high out of their minds on something so new, it wouldn't have shown up, because the doctors didn't know what to look for."

"It's possible, but I doubt it."

"And the rest of the troupe?"

"They've all been in and out of different institutions up and down the East coast."

"You're serious about this?"

"Some of them went into facilities for the criminally insane. Others are in psych wards, warning the staff of the coming of Hastur, or a second moon appearing in the sky, the stars turning black and the night sky turning a color they couldn't put a name to. Others hide panicked in the corner of the cells, insisting Hastur's minions are coming for them. The girl who played Cassilda insists she is the true queen of Aldonces and should be treated like a queen. The actor who played Thales, the elder son, is one of the most aggressive patients ever seen."

"You sure Sheilagh's dad wasn't punking you?"

"Sheilagh's dad works for the FBI," Lexus said, patiently.

"Like the government hasn't lied? What about MK-ULTRA?"

"That was the CIA."

"Meh, it's all the same. So what's at the bottom of this?"

"It's said that it has to do with the play they were performing. The text has been suppressed by several governments because reading it or performing it or even watching it was making people go crazy."

"Yeah, typical Fascist bullshit, telling us we can read anything except the books they tell us we can't read."

"Sheilagh's dad knows a guy who knows a lot about this ooga-booga stuff, so she asked him about it. He says it's bad news, that it's a coded ritual that summons some entity from another dimension."

"Yeah, right, makes people just think some kind of boogeyman is after them."

Lexus sighed, the line rustling, that odd pulse rising for a moment before she spoke again. "I'm only telling you what Sheilagh told me."

"Yeah, whatever. You coming over or not?"

"I got that paper due, and I don't think I'd better, if you plan to watch that thing."

"All right, I won't keep you. I'll tell you how it ends," he said, shutting off his phone before Lexus could say goodbye.

This time, he watched the tape more closely, keeping an eye out for the mystery figure, that strange face (if it was a face). No sign of it just yet, no more problems with the tape locking up. The story went on, of the fate of the kingdom on the shore of Lake Hali beneath its twin moons, the devotees of Hastur descending upon the last of House Aldonces. The story ended in a Grand Guignol denouement. He caught himself trying to figure out what techniques this bunch of amateurs could have used to pull it off. It convinced him more than the usual stage blood bags and cow tongue tactics these types tended to use.

It left such impression that the drama went on playing in the theater of his dreams, the insides of his eyelids the projector screen to catch the images. The red streaked figures in tattered garments, limping in procession along the dead shore of Lake Hali, the poisoned trees with their gnarled limbs stretched up to the sky, the two moons and the black sky with the even blacker stars mirrored on its surface, the darkness of the water rippling. The marchers cursed their fate, singing songs in strange keys, crying out wordless curses, emitting retching yowls, their bleeding faces and mouths streaming. The weaker marchers stumbled, falling, the stronger marchers trampling them, grinding their bleeding flesh into the dust of the roadbed.

Mason snapped awake, to sunlight glinting off a yellow school bus chugging below his bedroom window. He looked to his clock, the time telling him he was already late for a job interview at a public access cable station in Andover.

He had a feeling the job was toast even before it started, the way the assistant director asked him the questions in the most perfunctory voice. *I'll be stuck working grocery and helping Aunt Mel move clunky furniture the rest of my life,* he thought afterwards as he drove home. *Maybe I can get a gig making commercials for them.*

Busy day moving stuff out of the warehouse-barn behind Aunt Melanie's house and onto the shop floor that took up the whole downstairs, and he took a corner hard while helping her with a sideboard, clipping the back of it and swearing.

Aunt Melanie looked at him with concern. "You all right? You're crankier than usual."

"Yeah, had a rough time with the job interview," he said.

"You sure? You look pale. You coming down with something?"

The knotholes on the wood surface of the sideboard caught his attention, like the eye holes in a mask. He flinched visibly, he realized. "Had weird dreams last night, they kept me awake."

"That'll do it to you," she said, something in her voice sounding unconvinced. "You sure you're okay?

"Might be a bit jumpy over this job interview."

"I know someone you could talk to."

"I don't need a headshrinker, so much as I need a job."

"Well, talking to someone outside your usual sphere can help you feel less frayed about trying to get a job."

"As long as they don't mind me paying by sweeping their office floor or something."

Evening shift at the grocery store and Mason spent much of the time bagging or sweeping the floor. Something yellow shifted in his peripheral vision, causing him to jump and nearly knock over a woman's shopping basket on wheels with his broom handle.

"Watch where you're going," a woman in a yellow silk raincoat, pushing the shopping basket, snapped, shoving past him and muttering at the incompetence of the youngest generation.

"Get going yourself, you bat," Mason muttered.

That night brought more dreams, in which he pursued the ragged procession between ruined structures like crumbling castles and temples, bare trees lifting leafless branches to the dust-yellow sky above, more yellow dust rising in acrid puffs from under the marchers' feet where their blood had not yet clotted on the dusty road. He raised his eyes from this rabble to the sky above, to the skyline of the castle where House Aldonces had dwelt for generations, his to claim, as Hastur the kindly, Hastur the gracious, had promised, if he would present a fitting offering.

He jerked awake, the amber light on his alarm clock showing he had several hours left till he had to get up, but lay there unable to fall back to sleep

Next morning, he dragged himself through another shift at the antique shop. "I'll help you pay for a session with Doctor

Archer, if it helps," Aunt Mel offered. "If you can't sleep, this is all the reason you need."

"All right, all right, stop twisting my arm," Mason muttered.

She gave him the next day off, sending him to Dr. Archer's office. Mason could see why they would be friends: he could remember when the bookcases that lined the walls of the shrink's office had lined the walls in Aunt Mel's shop, holding up a bunch of Hummels she had trouble moving, along with some encyclopedias in cream colored bindings that had yellowed with age. Now they held up various thick manuals and binders, and a few framed photographs of forests and seasides, likely taken in Maine.

"It's a tough field to get into, I'm told," Dr. Archer, a small man, dark eyes behind silver-rimmed glasses, said. "I'm told there's a high demand for camera crew and film editors, but they're selective in who they hire."

"Too picky for their own good, if you ask me," Mason said.

Dr. Archer cocked his head, the light from the window glinting on his lenses. "You're feeling slightly on edge because it's taking so long to get a job in the field you chose."

"Who wouldn't feel this way? I take it this is the part where I break down bawling because I'll be bagging groceries and lugging furniture up staircases for my aunt, just to pay the bills, and where you reassure me that the right job is somewhere, I just have to be patient, yadda yadda yadda. Insert mommy-daddy-society wound talk."

"You really don't want to be here."

"The hell I don't. I should be out there, getting what's mine, my just deserves," Mason snapped, mind ticking back to the play, the elder son's rant in the first act.

"If you need to let it out, I'm here to listen," Dr. Archer said.

"No. I'm stressed, but I can take it."

"Well, what would care to talk about instead?"

"Nothing. Anything."

"What do you do when you're not working?"

"I watch a lot of movies. I know, cliché for an AV guy."

"Anything in particular?"

He told Archer about the box of VHS tapes, watching them with Lexus. He didn't mention the yellow label tape or the King in the Tattered Cloak. No point mentioning the dreams. He wasn't sure he wanted to go down that rabbit hole, and have this shrink tell him the dreams meant he really wanted to bang his aunt or something sick like that.

"So you critique these movies?

"Sort of. Point out what's bad production, learn what not to do. Think of things I'd do to improve it."

"Ah, so more than an MST3K session."

"That's some people's idea of movie critiquing, ain't mine. It's fun to watch when you want something goofy and brainless, but it's too snarky for my tastes."

"In that case, aside from some anxiety connected to the job search, I'd say you're doing well."

"So I don't have to come back?"

"If you feel the need, by all means, but otherwise, go forth and prosper, young man.

The light on the answering machine blinked when Mason got home. He played back the message.

"Thank you for your application. We're still reviewing it with all due consideration...." Yaddah, yaddah, yaddah, usual HR blather.

Off to work at the grocery that night, despite the set back. The usual crowd came through: stay at home moms or second shift moms coming in with their ankle biters in tow. Including one not yet old enough for school using the carriage as climbing bars.

"Ma'am, can you not let your child clamber on the carriage?" the words slipping out of Mason's mouth before he could stop them.

"He's not bothering you. Kids need to climb and exercise," Mommie said.

"Yeah, but they're in my way as I repack your carriage." Mason reached over and around the kid hanging from the side of the carriage. He swore the kid moved right into his path to get into his path on purpose. Grabbing a bag with several boxes in it, Mason slung it into the carriage, clipping the kid's shoulder. The kid jumped off the carriage, running to his mother for comfort.

"We got in each other's way," Mason said.

"You did that on purpose," Mommie said, pulling her pup close.

"Wasn't trying to," Mason said, proving her point.

Mommie paid the bill, but rather than going on her way, she approached Petersen the assistant front end manager, talked to him in a low voice.

At Mason's break, Petersen took him aside. "What happened with that kid and a bag of cereal boxes?" he asked.

"What about what kid and a bag of cereal boxes?"

"A woman says you hit her son with a bag of cereal boxes," Petersen said, looking him in the eye. "Was it an accident?"

"Of course it was an accident. You take me for the kind of man who beats kids?"

"You've been a bit more grouchy than you usually are."

"I just got the run around from a job I applied to. It'd put anyone on edge."

"If your attitude here was anything like your attitude at your interview, I can see why they might be reluctant to hire you," Petersen said.

"Whatever. I need coffee," Mason said.

First customer after his break, an old woman who reeked of perfume she'd drenched herself in to cover her stale, unwashed stench. Mason reached up to pinch his nose shut while bagging her groceries – packages of cupcakes and cans of cat food – with the other.

"Don't make the bag so heavy," she said, her S's squeaking through her dentures, as he put a single jar of mayonnaise into one plastic sack and set it aside to open the next bag.

"There's only one thing in these bags," Mason said.

"Don't contradict me, young man."

"Ma'am, with all respect due to your dotage, there is only one thing in each of these bags or two to three very light things. If you see more than one jar in that bag, you need your eyes checked."

"Don't talk to me like that! How dare you speak so disrespectful to a poor old widder woman," the hag snapped, as she raised her cane to brandish it at Mason.

How dare she speak to me like that, he thought and grabbed the cane, yanking it from her gnarled fingers and swiping at her with it. The hag screamed one of those overwrought old beldame screams and staggered backward into the commoner behind her.

He swiped the cane at her head. She shuffled out of the way. "Come back to me, you harridan!" Mason cried, one part of his mind puzzling at his vocabulary before his rage throttled this brief voice of concern. He lunged across the end of the register at her. She shuffled backward, falling into a shopping carriage behind her. The customer hauled the cart backward as Mason reached for her.

"What's going on?" - "The bagging kid's gone crazy" - "Someone find a manager!" - The rest of the line and the customers in the aisle behind them scuttled backward before some turned to run. Mason swiped at the nearest person with his cudgel. How dare they address a member of House Aldonces in such a manner. Let these peasants cower and snivel, he would give them reason to mewl as they did.

A heavy hand fell upon his shoulder. He looked over, his mind briefly registering Famolare, the store director, till he fell back to himself, awakening to the mask falling away, to gaze upon this minion of the dread King, Hastur the Unspeakable, Hastur come to wrench the crown from the heirs of Camilla.

He swung the cudgel to drive off the vile minion, but it wrenched the weapon from his hands. Emitting a war cry, he lunged at the minion. It seized him and dragged him down into the darkness as his head cracked on the yellow floor tiles...

Yellowvator

(Enquiry Remix)

"Come on, the Biltmore is perfect for this kind of ritual," Chelsee said, throwing her arm around her friend and roommate Michaela's shoulders, as she tried to unpack her suitcase.

Michaela pulled from under Chelsee's arm and walked to the hotel room bureau with an armload of tee shirts. "A hotel that's supposedly haunted? There were eleven murders here. People have disappeared randomly, the last one was about five years ago." The weekend at WeirdCon in Providence, Rhode Island promised to be a blast, but Michaela knew her caution likely would take at least a tiny bit out of their metaphoric sails. As long as it didn't hurt sales of a different variety, namely, her books, or Chelsee's jewelry in the dealer room several floors below them.

"I just want to see if it's true, if it really works," Chelsee said. "There's plenty of YouTube vids where it doesn't work."

Michaela pushed the drawer shut with her hip before going to the cardboard-reinforced canvas bag containing her books, which sat in a corner of the hotel room. "That's why you don't see it working: If it did work and it worked too well, I doubt anyone would want to post it. And then there's the people who supposedly didn't make it back and wouldn't be able to post it."

"You mean like the guy in Memphis who disappeared and turned up on the roof of an apartment building? I thought most people figured he probably wasn't playing the Elevator Ritual, only that he got messed up with some drug dealers in the area," Chelsee said.

Michaela chuckled dryly. "And aren't you the one who likes to keep all the possibilities in mind?"

"I'd like to think that someone with her medical problems didn't have that added to it." Chelsee said. "Hey, I'll pay for your dinner if you do this with me,"

Michaela chuckled low in her throat. "Now you're fighting dirty." Her lifelong chum disliked paying much for meals, and it was one way to make sure the budding writer didn't spend the entire four day weekend living off Starbucks and Dunkin Donuts. "All right, I'll do it. But please don't beg me to do anything like this again."

They went down several floors to the hallway that served as a kind of stretched-out dealers' room, to set up their shared table. A few early-bird convention-goers approached, some passing by, some lingering to buy some of Chelsee's refurbished vintage rings and a copy or two of Michaela's poetry chapbooks.

Jim Maitland, one of the con organizers, came down the corridor at one point, a clipboard in hand, his sandy hair on end and his usually natty black shirt and maroon vest combo rumpled. "How are you girls settling in?"

"As you can see, we got the table ready for the weekend, and we're planning to have dinner later and take in a show," Michaela said.

"As long as she makes good to help me do the Elevator Ritual later," Chelsee said, nudging Michaela's shoulder with hers. Michaela threw her a Look for that.

Jim blinked at them, giving Chelsee a concerned stare. "I'm not sure I'd mess around with the Elevator Ritual, not here anyway. Maybe across the way at the Omni Hotel."

"Why not? Are those old Mob stories true?" Chelsee teased.

"The place is haunted, and I can attest to this personally," Jim said. "Peta and I spent our anniversary in one of the suites here. The bathroom door kept opening for no reason at all. Then about three in the morning, something walked across our pillows. Peta jumped out of bed and tore it apart, looking for whatever disturbed us."

"Don't tell me the place has rats," Michaela groaned.

"No, as far as we could tell. We found no traces of rats: no holes in the walls, nothing. We called the desk, and they moved us to another room. Apparently the hotel has had trouble with that room in particular, but we managed to sleep the rest of that night in the new room. But since then, I've bunked at the Omni during WeirdCon.

"You know that the financier who backed the construction on the Biltmore was involved in dark magic? Supposedly he and his business cronies performed some strange rituals in the main ballroom," Jim added.

"Wonder if any familiars are still lurking around the hallways," Chelsee said.

"This makes the Elevator Ritual even less of a good idea," Michaela said.

"You said it might not even work anyway," Chelsee said. "If nothing else, maybe it'll give you an idea for a new story."

"Yeah, about a convention goer who bugs her best friend to insanity," Michaela twitted back.

"Either way, enjoy the convention and stay safe. I'll talk with you somewhere along the way," Jim said, before moving on.

A couple of hours later, around six, the girls covered their table with some black tablecloths and went down to the mezzanine level.

In a smaller ballroom, they took in a half staged performance of *The Tattered King*, a Robert W Chambers-inspired play, capped off by an actor gliding in from the back of the audience, clad in a ragged yellow robe, surmounted with a pale face mask completely covering their face and a pair of antlers on a headband. The sight of the intruder startled one glasses-wearing brunette girl with a "Straight out of Dunwich" shirt right out of her chair, and caused more than a few others in the audience to scream in shock even while they clapped.

After drinks and appetizers in the hotel restaurant (which according to Chelsee looked like the perfect setting for a Prohibition-era Mob show, with its brass and mahogany fixtures and Art Nouveau details), the two girls hung out in the hotel lobby, chatting with each other as they watched the passersby coming and going, till the hotel started to quiet down toward midnight. The night desk clerk came to relieve the evening clerk, and the canned electro-swing playing on the lobby seemed louder, more distinct.

A group of business people in suits crossed the lobby to the elevators, looking a bit rumpled and travel weary, and got onto the car on the far left. Chelsee waited until the doors closed on the interlopers before she walked to the elevator on the far right, and hit the down button. Deep inside the wall, the motor whirred and rumbled into motion.

"I think this was the elevator I almost got stuck in during the last WeirdCon, with that *ReAnimator* guy, and a bunch of college guys from Germany," Michaela said,

"Got stuck in? That sounds awful," Chelsee said.

"It wasn't so bad: it just stopped suddenly and we thought we'd have to hit the call button for help," Michaela said. "But it started right up again, right when we started getting antsy."

"Which *ReAnimator* guy? The writer guy, or the little guy with the glasses?" Chelsee asked. At that moment, the elevator doors pinged open. Chelsee stepped into the gilt-accented interior with its dusky mirror-like walls. Michaela glanced around, as if worried someone might see them, then stepped into the elevator. The doors slid shut behind her.

"So now what do we do?" Michaela said, stepping back from the panel of buttons.

Chelsee tapped the button for the sixth floor. "So you press the button for the sixth floor, like I just did, then the twelfth, then the sixth floor again, then the eighth, then you hit the button for the ground floor. The elevator should bring you to the ground floor, then suddenly head for the twelfth floor without stopping. The door should open and everything will look black and white instead of colored."

"Isn't there something about a person getting on at some point?" Michaela asked.

"Yeah, a girl is supposed to get on when you reach the lobby," Chelsee said, hitting the twelfth floor button. The elevator started moving.

"We'll see if a girl gets on," Michaela said.

"What would you do if a girl did get on?" Chelsee asked with a conspiratorial smirk.

"Probably not pay her much attention. It's a hotel during a convention. Someone's likely to get on, even at a weird hour like this."

Chelsee hit the sixth floor button again. The elevator dropped. "Good call. Every version I've heard says you shouldn't talk to or look at the girl if she gets on."

"Why? What happens if you do talk to her?" Michaela folded her arms across her chest.

"Every version I've heard says you won't make it back safely. She's supposedly a messenger from the spirit world, and if you talk to her, the spirits will snatch you away."

"Well, that's weird. If she's a messenger, what if she has a message for you?"

Chelsee hit the twelfth floor button. With a creak, the elevator rose. "I guess if she has something to say to you, you listen but you don't look at her, or reply to her."

"Still sounds more than a bit inconsistent, but whatever," Michaela said.

Chelsee hit the ground floor button. The doors slid shut and the car sank. It stopped. The doors slid open, revealing a young woman a shade older than either of the girls, wearing a long, sleeveless yellow dress. She stepped into the elevator. Michaela, despite her misgivings, averted her eyes. Chelsee let out a small, excited, nervous chitter, nudging Michaela before dropping her own gaze to the floor of the elevator.

The car hesitated. Then with a mechanical creak and a groan deep in the wall behind the car they started ascending. *I expected as much,* Michaela thought. *This girl is probably just some Robert*

W Chambers fan, who's wearing a yellow dress in honor of her favorite book of weird stories, probably on her way back to her room for a good night's sleep. And Chelsee probably hit the twelfth floor button when I got distracted by the girl getting on. But she kept her gaze toward her own shoes nevertheless.

Chelsee gasped and reached for Michaela's arm. "It's happening. It's really happening.", they climbed again.

Michaela wanted to say, 'It could be happening because you pressed so many buttons in succession', but she held her tongue. The woman in yellow remained stolidly silent and unmoved, gauging by her reflection in the walls of the car.

When the red number 12 appeared on the digital indicator panel above the buttons, the elevator juddered to a stop. The doors remained shut, not even shifting as if they might open.

. The doors shifted, then hesitated, then dragged open onto a blindingly white hallway. Michaela blinked, raising her arm to shield her eyes. The woman in yellow beside them had vanished, no way she could simply have walked out. Even without either of them looking at her directly, they would have noticed her departing.

Chelsee scampered out into the hallway, so unlike the softly lit cream-colored hallways with burnt umber, green and gold accents found everywhere else in the Biltmore.

"Chels, don't go far," Michaela warned.

"This sure doesn't look like a typical floor," Chelsee said.

Michaela would have said, 'No shit, Sherlock' except that her brain started to check out. "Oh God," she murmured.

"It worked!" Chelsee said, stepping further into the hallway proper.

"Chelsee, don't go too far," Michaela said, staying inside the elevator.

"I'm just going to the end of the hallway and back, I promise," Chelsee said over her shoulder as she walked away down the hall.

Michaela could not watch her friend wander off and so she followed her.

The air echoed. One couldn't say they heard noises. The air itself seemed to generate the noise, a weird vibration, not musical, not tonal, not voices, not animal calls, not mechanical rumbles or clinks, not human voices. Black doors with transom windows above them lined the hallway, much as they did a typical hallway in the hotel, except the doors looked as though someone had made them from the shells of insects or prehistoric sea creatures.

"Wow, this place, it's like the bizarro Biltmore," Chelsee said.

"Yeah, sure is, Can we go back?"

"Just to the end of the hallway," Chelsee wheedled.

Something scratched behind a door, like claws on shells. A creak like straining floorboards rose behind another. A door up ahead creaked and cracked, bowing out, then bending inward, as if the door breathed.

"Let's get out of here," Michaela said.

"Like I said, just to the end of the hallway. We're almost there," Chelsee pleaded.

The hallway twisted at an odd angle, the further they progressed, more corkscrew than elbow. Somehow they kept their feet on the black and white tessellated floor, but Michaela felt her head spin as they continued.

Up ahead, a window came into view, a window opening onto a view of the city, not the scattering of high rises and tree tops and roofs of houses, but oddly peaked roofs and bulbous domes. Where the sun or the moon should have hovered, a strange yellow shape like a scorpion hung in the blindingly white sky, black stars wheeling about it in unfamiliar constellations, unknown to Earth.

"I guess we're in bizarro Providence," Chelsee said.

"If it is Providence," Michaela said. A name, a phrase rose in her mind: *Hali, on the shore of the dead lake...*

"Let's go back," Chelsee said. Michaela's heart rose in her chest. They turned to go back. Something banged the inside of one door. Chelsee yipped and ran for the elevator.

"Chels, don't run!" Michaela yelled, running after her friend.

The elevator came into sight. One of the hall doors nearest to Chelsee crackled and bowed out, a membrane stretched over a limb, sprouting digits, tendrils ending in talons, that reached even farther. Chelsee froze in her tracks, like a deer caught in a train's headlight, staring at it. Michaela grabbed Chelsee's hand, and rushed her toward the elevator.

Michaela fell into the elevator. Chelsee screamed. Propping herself on her elbow, Michaela looked back. The talon-tendril wrapped about Chelsee's torso, drawing her away from the open elevator door.

Michaela braced her knees on the floor, and rose, grabbing Chelsee's arm with both hands.

"Let go, you're hurting me," Chelsee pleaded.

"Not leaving you here," Michaela said.

The talon-tendril tightened, pulling on Chelsee. Michaela's shoulder creaked as she pulled back. She whined in pain, but pulled with all her strength.

Something tore with a sucking, wet noise. She fell backward into the elevator, hearing Chelsee fall to the floor behind her. Michaela reached up and punched the Lobby button on the elevator panel. She looked down to Chelsee and screamed, seeing the blood covering her friend's body, where the talon-tendril had ripped through her clothes.

The doors slid shut. Something slapped the doors outside, but they descended.

The elevator slid to a halt, doors sliding open. A cluster of people, some in evening dress, some in costumes, stood before them. When they looked into the elevator, they backed up, some whimpering in fear, others gasping in disgust.

"Someone dial 911!" - "Is there a doctor here?" - "What happened to these girls?" -"Is that blood on the floor?"

"I think we need some help," Michaela said, looking down at Chelsee, laying puddled at her feet.

In a room in a hospital in Providence, Michaela lay curled in the bed, still in shock from what happened.

The nurse who'd tended to her entered, followed by two men in suits, one tall, broad-shouldered and dark looked as if he should be breaking kneecaps for the Mob, the other shorter, slight but lightly muscled, and blond, wearing steel-rimmed glasses, looked like a misplaced professor.

"Michaela, these gentlemen are from the FBI," the nurse said. "If you feel up for it, they'd like to talk to you about what happened at the Biltmore."

The two agents introduced themselves, showing her their credentials. The shorter agent held his billfold in a delicate hand clad in a fingerless black leather driving glove. The taller agent drew one of the room chairs to the head of the bed and seated himself, while the other remained standing at the foot of the bed, hands clasped low before him.

"Were you aware of the number of people who have disappeared from the Biltmore Hotel in recent years?" the shorter Fed asked.

"Heard that bad things went on there." She hesitated, hoping her answer satisfied them. "Thought it had to do with the Mob. Providence is a Mob city, isn't it?"

The taller Fed nodded. "It is, not as much as it used to be, but there's still some wiseguys around town. Used to handle organized crime cases. Even put away some guys I grew up with before the Bureau teamed me up with this little weirdo." The shorter Fed cleared his throat sharply, darting a Look at his colleague.

"Must have been hard, having to get tough with a friend,"

"They broke the law. I had to help turn the wheels of justice," the taller Fed said.

"So all those people who disappeared, it had to do with the Mob, right? Chelsee saw something she shouldn't and they whacked her, right? What we saw, that was some kind of drugs they put in the ventilation?"

The shorter Fed replied slowly, weighing his words. "Not all of them, no. The two of you were in an elevator most of the time. Chelsee was pushing buttons in a certain order, wasn't she?"

"She was. A girl got on. She vanished. I mean, the girl."

"There was a security camera in the elevator. A girl never got on with you," the taller Fed said, almost apologizing.

"There was!" Michaela insisted, her temples throbbing. "There was a girl in a yellow dress."

"If anything, the camera cut out for about five minutes after it stopped and before it showed you dragging Chelsee back into the elevator.", the shorter Fed said.

"We stopped after the girl got on. We stopped on this... bizarro floor and the girl in yellow disappeared. You have to believe me."

"You saw it, though, didn't you? You saw the spirit world? You walked through it, didn't you?" the shorter Fed asked,

"We got off on a hallway. We'd walked to the end, and Chelsee... Chelsee..." She couldn't stop her tears, her body shaking from sobs, panting....

"She saw it?" the taller Fed asked, his voice, his words a lifeline tossed into the spiral of anxiety and horror she dropped into.

"I saw it. She went to look at it, in the window. Told her not to go there. No... no, don't go there, don't keep walking there, go back."

"Then what happened?" the shorter Fed asked.

"Something in a doorway grabbed her. I grabbed her arm. It pulled her in. I still hung onto her, though I couldn't... couldn't save..."

"No one could, not when they were against something like that," the shorter Fed said. The taller one gave her a Look. Oh, he knew, he knew, the smaller man knew, he knew it was true.

"Is she all right?" she asked. "Did she get out safe?"

The two agents exchanged glances in silence, then looked to her, the taller Fed speaking. "She didn't make it. I'm sorry. Her injuries were too severe."

It was true. She knew, it was true. Oh swell, oh hell, oh yellow in the elevator, cut the cord, falling falling falling falling free why she? why me? why was it she? who made it free? why did it have to be Chelsee? why couldn't it be me in the hell, in the yellow hell elevator? oh God oh no oh no...

Everything slid sideways, flying hospital trays and the tall Fed jumping to his feet, catching, caught her, catching her as she fell down a well, as she fell into her own yell from hell...

"Poor girl, she's seen the Yellow Sign," the shorter Fed said.

Grand Staircase to the Yellow Court

(Overexposed Remix)

"So why's Halsey giving you the fresh air beat?" Melinda asked, drumming the tips of her index fingers on the steering wheel as we buzzed along Route 114 through Middleton, her Ford Escort wagon carrying us past a jumble of feed stores and antique shops, catering to the motley population here on the border between Middlesex and Essex counties.

I cranked a new roll of film into my Agfa. "Said the change of pace would do me good. Besides, it helps you put that Local History training to good use. I've wanted your help on a project for a long time."

"Yeah, and I kept being a brat and turning you down, the other times you asked for my help," she said.

"You grew up this past year."

She darted an annoyed smirk, more smirk than annoyance, to me. "If that came from anyone but you, Uncle Carton, I'd stop and let them walk the rest of the way to the woods." She stuck her tongue out at my reflection in the rear view mirror, but her eyes winked at me.

She glanced to the autumn foliage that flickered past us, framing the shops and houses. "I'm serious, though. What got you interested in checking out a legend based on something out in the woods? I didn't think you went in for the ooga-booga shift? Or has working in 'witch-haunted Salem' warmed you up to the local color?"

I slid the camera into the foam matrix on the case at my feet in the floorboards, and took out another one to load it. "Could be part of it. The rest could be this one intrigued me when I first heard it whispered about."

"Intrigued enough to get you tromping through a woods?" She glanced at me from under her beret. "It's the staircase story."

"You heard of it?"

She chaffed softly. "Half the kids in History at Merrimack College have gone traipsing through the woods, looking for it when they've had a few at a kegger. The other two take their classes too serious to give it a second thought."

"Have you seen it?"

"No." She paused, darting a look to me. "Well, not yet."

"So I take it, you were in Group B, but a friend in Group A dragged you along?"

Busted. She blushed. "Yeah, my friend Jared and his drama club buddies talked me into it. It was dripping rain. We went in through the back entrance of the forest, and I lost a shoe, so we turned back."

I peered out the window to the clear blue sky above us. "All the more reason to hitch a ride with you: you've been here before."

She chaffed. "Uncle Carton, I was here in the dark. That's a whole other beast from going there in the day."

"It is and it isn't. Also, it gives you a chance to see what you missed."

Her annoyed look softened, and she glanced from the road to me, a small smile of quiet gratitude quirking her mouth, alongside the pink that showed in her cheeks.

We made the hairpin turn where 114 merges with Boston Street and followed it, the road lined with a double row of tall white pines, till we came to the State Police station, with the entrance to the Harold Parker State Forest immediately to the left of it. We pulled into the drive leading into the forest, going in a good half a mile under the trees before we reached a ranger station and a parking area, with a picnic area beyond it, under a stand of pines where the park had cleared the bracken and bushes. The one young ranger we spoke to hinted that the staircase might be found about a half a mile off the main road, but the older ranger who appeared to be his superior shook her head at him as if in warning. I paid the parking fee and the two of us stepped into the woods.

We followed what looked like an old logging road or a road to a house that had once stood secluded in the woods, the edges softened by new growth and bracken. Golden sunlight angled through the thinning canopy of maples, the oaks just starting to turn russet against the ever green of the pines. I took a few fluff shots looking up at the underside of the branches, the clear blue sky shining through the gaps left by the fallen leaves.

We crossed a small stream over a bridge made from three thick fallen trees, braced among the remains of small stone pylons on the banks, what had once supported a bridge.

"Odd how far it is into the woods. If it was part of a house, I'd think it would be closer to the road," Melinda said.

I looked away from lining up a shot of a large pine cone in the midst of a spray of needles on the end of a branch, waiting for the breeze to stop swaying it. "It is, though considering some of the legends I've heard, it wouldn't surprise me if something in the forest is pushing it back or simply growing over it."

"What, if it isn't nature, it's some kind of time-space thing? You watching that show with the crazy FBI agent?"

"Which one, the one who likes his damn fine coffee?" I held my breath, releasing it when I hit the shutter.

"No, the new one with the aliens and the brainy partner with the red hair."

I spooled the film. "Can't say I have. What stories have you heard?"

"The one going around school, they say the house belonged to a rich family in the 1820s. The daughter was supposed to inherit the house and the land, if she married well. She didn't intend to marry, and so her father tried to arrange a match. But she turned down every single one. Her father then locked her away in the attic of the house. She went stir crazy and he planned to send her to the madhouse at the East Manuxet State Hospital, or the one in Danvers – depending on who's telling the story. But that never happened, because..." she paused for dramatic effect. "One night, she threw herself into the fire on the hearth in her rooms, and with her clothing all aflame, she ran screaming through the halls of the house, setting it ablaze, till nothing remained but a marble staircase that ran down the middle of the house."

I tucked the Agfa back into the case and took out the Nikon, draping the strap around my neck as we pressed on. "Sounds a lot like one of the subplots in *Jane Eyre*."

"Yeah, I thought that the first time I heard it. Though who's to say that the first Mrs. Rochester didn't have a real life counterpart?

"So what did you hear?"

"I'd heard from friends at the Essex Institute that the house belonged to an eccentric heiress, Miss Sherry Bainbridge, who'd built it as her country retreat. She'd come up to Boston to beat the summer heat or just to get away from the city, to entertain a circle of artists and poets and other bohemian types. They'd put on theatricals in the summer, at least till Miss Sherry started to fade and lose her spirit. She went to a doctor in New York, who diagnosed her with lung cancer. While she was gone but before her passing, the house caught fire under mysterious circumstances, as if it consumed itself out of grief."

"...And all that remains is an intact stone staircase leading into thin air," she concluded dramatically. "I think I like your version better."

The aspens along the path opened up into a great clearing, littered with bits of stone poking up through the leaf mold at our feet, like the bones of a fallen beast. My mind flicked to the Time-Life *Enchanted World* books on my friend Irena's shelves, an image in their "Giants and Dwarves", of the creation of Midgard from the body of the frost giant Ymir, bits of bones and jaw and vertebrae sticking up from the earth. Before us, in the midst of secondary growth oaks, about seventy or eighty years old, rose the staircase in a curve away from us and toward the trees, as if leading into them, the steps clear of fallen leaves, no trace of moss or lichen growing on them either, no acorns or nutshells, no signs of animal scat, as if no living thing would linger near them for long. Time had worn the edges of the stone risers, but not as much as one would expect. I supposed that someone could have come and cleaned them recently, but something in my gut hinted this was not the case. Not a breath of wind disturbed the leaves. Any bird sounds came from the distance.

"Whoa," she murmured, pausing behind me. I raised my camera, adjusted the focus, racked the zoom on the lens and took the first of several shots.

"Hey," she said, her voice like a rock tossed into still waters.

I jumped a bit, inside my work vest. "Huh?"

"Mind if I get into a shot? Make it a bit more human interest-y or give you a size comparison? People won't get a good idea of the scale otherwise."

"You could stand in front of them, but I wouldn't try walking up them, just to be safe." Even as I said this, she crunched through the leaves, approached the steps and climbed up three of them before I could object. I eyed the airy quasi-Gothic arches that seemed to just barely support the steps.

Melinda turned toward me, spreading her arms gracefully, reminiscent of the portrait of Isabella Stewart Gardner descending a staircase, though her tweed jacket and jeans certainly didn't resemble Madame Gardner's flowing white gown. I snapped several shots, while the sunlight caught on her just so. Melinda shifted her pose, maintaining that dramatic grace, turning Gloria Swanson-esque, in a way meant to say she was "ready for [her] close-up", though I'm certainly no Mr. DeMille.

At one point, she glanced over her shoulder, eyes widening. She turned back, stepping down toward me. I clicked the shutter at that split second, the shot taking on the look of a Seventies Gothic romance cover.

"Mel, you trying to look like Lady Davenport fleeing from her ghostly pursuer?" I asked.

"Too close," she said, little louder than a whisper.

I cranked the film to the end, took out the roll and slotted it into an empty 35mm container before tucking it into one of the many pockets in my vest. "What?"

She stepped behind me, putting me between herself and the staircase. "I don't know. Maybe it was the light through the foliage, but I thought I saw a shape floating through the trees,"

"Maybe there's more to those stories than people trying to get a scare out of each other," I said, looking to the tree tops. Those clouds that often roll in, during an October afternoon, had started gathering. "We are burning daylight."

"Got enough shots?" she asked.

"Got quite a few good ones. I might save the Gothic romance cover for a gallery image," I said. "Maybe enter it into the Topsfield Fair's photography show. 'The Secret of the Staircase.'"

"Don't you dare call it that." Her eyes were still wide and her smile hadn't returned. Something had spooked her hard.

I found what had spooked her when I got the film back to my Salem apartment, in a house where Nathaniel Hawthorne once lived on Federal Street.

Most of the shots came out well, but the light must have gone weird on one of the *Sunset Boulevard* shots, and I might have moved when I thought I hadn't. A squiggle of light, almost like three pothooks joined at the non-business end, turned up in one shot, hovering over Melinda's head. Then in another, a misty shape like a figure appeared behind Melinda. I looked at the negatives on my light box, even made another print, blown up, to get a better look at it.

In the third image, where Melinda had looked back, the figure looked even clearer, manifesting like a tall form in a hooded robe seeming to hover behind her. I wonder if a spirit attached to the land had made itself present, but I doubted that. After I'd snapped a witch blown into Salem on the winds of the No-Name Hurricane the previous autumn, I should have braced myself for anything weird, come this time of year, but this could be harder to prove as anything more than a trick of the light.

I delivered the shots the next morning. Halsey grumbled at some of the "more artsy-tartsy" shots, but he earmarked some of the earlier shots of the staircase by itself and of Melinda standing on the lower steps for future publication, once I delivered the article.

That night, I called Melinda, wanting to talk to her about. Her roommate picked up, then quickly put her on.

"*Hey, Uncle Carton,*" she said, sounding tired.

"Hey there, Mel. Been hitting the books, or are the books hitting you back?"

"*Something like that.*" She managed a laugh as she spoke.

"About yesterday, I'm sorry I teased you about getting spooked." And I told her what I'd seen in the pictures. "It's probably an anomaly in the film, or the light refracting through the leaves, but maybe the film picked up something. My brain might have filtered it out when I took the pictures."

"Maybe. You busy tomorrow? I've been doing some digging around, and I found out the reality behind those stories."

"I can free up a few hours in the afternoon."

"Good. Can we meet in that sandwich shop across from the Derby Square Book Store?"

I penciled it into my planner. "Sure thing."

The next day, over paninis and tea at the Witch City Cafe, Melinda laid out some printouts from the Andover Library microfilm.

"You were closer to the truth when you told your version of the story," she said. "There was a house there in the 1850s, the country home of Hiram Cabot, a textile baron, and Camilla Jaquith-Cabot his wife, who'd been an actress, spent a lot of time there. She gathered some of her friends from her former acting troupe and started putting on small shows at the country house. Hiram grew suspicious, in case she might be getting busy with her male co-actors, and so he started bringing some of his colleagues to spend the weekends at the house.

"Then one night in autumn, the troupe decided to put on a new play recently translated from the French, *Le Roi Jaune,* The play was a success, in the sense that the audience fully enjoyed it, but in another way, it was too successful."

"Do I want to know what you mean by 'too successful'? Audience participation got a little too real?"

She gave a Look that brooked no joking. "The actors continued the show, after the curtain dropped, still playing at being members of the court of Queen Camilla of the decayed, decadent kingdom of Yhtill."

"So it turned into a LARP?"

She pointed to a paragraph in the middle of the sheet. "Read that."

"'House servants who escaped before the final immolation appeared as frightful shadows of men and women described the final days of madness. Both the players and their audience could no longer be discerned for all sought out whatever bits of yellow fabric they could lay hands on, even tearing up great pieces of fabric from the drapes upon the windows and the upholstery upon the couches and chairs of the Yellow Sitting Room, with which to deck themselves. They chattered among themselves, not as players performing, but like children at play fully convinced that they were the court of Queen Camilla, awaiting the rise of lost Carcosa. "It was not so strange at first. It reminded me of a book that my sister had read to me, about a man who thought himself a knight and rode about the land thinking two flocks of sheep were armies in battle, or a peasant girl was a queen," said one kitchen maid. A houseboy described the 'fancy folk' whispering among themselves of a 'Yellow King' who would arrive.

"'On the third night after the performance, according to the word of the maid, the actors and even the guests began to act as though the King walked in their midst, bowing to something that the servants, who hadn't attended the play, could not see.

"'At length, in a mad ecstasy, speaking as if they did the bidding of the unseen King, they fell upon each other, mauling each other in ways that no civil person can describe. Still living despite their injuries, they turned upon the servants, who fled into the forest that surrounds the house. As they fled, several lamps were overturned and spilled out the oil, soaking the rugs and drapes and spreading the flames. Some of the maddened guests walked into the flames, chaunting in mad ecstasy, till they set the entire house ablaze.

"'The manservant to the master of the house, who had already fled into the garden, looked back to behold the lady of the house, with her garments all ablaze, stepping out upon the landing of the stone staircase that lead to the upper story of the house, gliding down as if she leaned upon the arm of her king and lord, before she collapsed upon the lawn.'"

We sat in silence, til the paper rustled as I laid the pages on the table. "Frightening," I said.

She straightened the pages, her hands quivering. "Probably mass hysteria."

"There may have been something to it," I said, reaching into my case for the envelope containing my photographs, laying them out next to her printouts.

She pulled them close, studying the images. After a moment, she edged back in her chair, as if getting away from something invading her personal space, but she pointed to the image with the indistinct figure. "That's... is that...?"

"It looked regal to me."

"The face looks like a mask."

"Or a skull."

"Or the mask is the skull," said a male voice, close to the table. Melinda looked up to a tousle-headed young man about her age, holding a thick red-rope envelope. Melinda quickly introduced me to one of her friends in the English Lit cum drama club, Jared Plympton.

He held up the envelope. "Took some digging, but I found that play you talked about." He opened it and drew out a paperback with a worn brown cover, the middle of the front bearing an emblem like the tails of three scorpions joined at the root, printed in yellow.

Melinda reared back, like a cat startled by an intrusive dog. "Jared, I said I'd read more about that thing than I cared to. That didn't mean I wanted to read the book itself."

I gave the book a hard look. "I'm not sure I'd want to get near it neither, after hearing what a performance did to the audience."

"Aw, come on, those old newspapers used to exaggerate stuff all the time," Jared argued.

"Have you even read it?" Melinda asked.

"I skimmed through the first act: typical post-Shakespeare stuff," Jared said. "It's not like I got the drama group putting it on for the Halloween party. I thought your uncle here could use it for his research."

"I think I've heard enough about it," I said.

Jared returned the book to his envelope, and I could swear the air got warmer as soon as he did. "Well, I guess I can give it back to my aunt's friend in the library at Philips Academy."

Halsey sent my photos and the copy I'd cranked out, with Melinda credited as my research assistant, to the press, intending to run it as a "Local Legend" on the travel page of the Saturday late edition, on Halloween. I thought nothing more about it the next few days, my recollection of the book and the staircase buried under the detritus of photographing Haunted Happenings events.

Til the night before Halloween, late in the evening while a light rain tapped at the windows, as I finished preparing a set of proofs for delivery, when someone pounded on the hall door to my apartment.

"Tell Halsey the shots are in the can, and they'll be right down," I called out, thinking it was the courier already arrived.

"Uncle Carton, open up!" Melinda's voice called.

I dropped the proof sheets onto my work table and ran to the door. Melinda stood in the hallway, trying to keep from shaking, her face white as the proverbial ghost.

"What's happened?" I asked.

"It's Jared. He and the drama club... they're in the Harold Parker Forest. I think they're putting on the play."

"In the woods? On a night like this?"

"They got the bug, and it bit them hard. Jared snooped in my notes, told his goofy friends. They think it's all a joke."

"Let's go snap them out of it." I went for my cheapest waterproof camera and several rolls of film. I was not about to let this go undocumented.

We drove to Harold Parker Forest as quickly as we dared and the rain slick roads would allow. We practically ditched the car in the visitor's parking lot. Someone, likely the forest rangers spooked by the intruders, had tipped off the police: a battle line of cars from Andover, Middleton, East Manuxet and elsewhere lined the road, their red and blue beacons strobing off the trees and casting wavering shadows. A K-9 unit had joined them, the dogs with their handlers following at the end of their leads going into the trees.

A burly officer standing a head taller than Melinda and a full head and shoulders taller than I approached us, flashlight in hand, his face cast in shadow. "You can't go in there."

I held up my press pass on its lanyard. "Sure I can." The cop studied the pass, then looked to Melinda. "My research assistant. She got the tip."

The cop shot Melinda a dubious scowl, then stepped aside. "All right, but keep back. Kids get into this Satan stuff and who knows what could happen?" He lead us under the dripping canopy of the trees, the rain falling through the branches more easily than it would have a half a month ago.

Torchlight shone through the trees, the light sputtering fitfully. Tree trunks rose up around us like the colonnade of an old castle or a cathedral. Voices rose, declaiming their measured lines.

"*Indeed it's time. We all have laid aside disguise but you*," a woman's voice declared.

"*I wear no mask*," a male voice replied, hollowly, as if speaking through a mask.

"*No mask? No mask!*" a female voice spoke, in what sounded like a terrified aside.

The clearing where the Cabot house had stood, where the staircase remained opened up before us. Those torches we'd seen stood at the corners of the space, some already doused by the rain. The police had formed a cordon around the space, their captains arguing with a slightly older student, who appeared to be in charge.

At the foot of the staircase, a group of students stood arrayed in cobbled-together robes in bright, even saturated colors with matching party-store domino masks on their faces. A figure that resembled Jared knelt before a figure in yellow, with a white and gold mask on its face. It held a blade that didn't look like a prop over Jared's head, as it tilted his head back, its hand cupping the back of his head.

The police shouted to the masked figure to drop the knife, but she (he?) lowered the blade closer, point downwards, toward Jared's face.

Melinda broke loose from the police line, ducking under my arm. She rushed the stage, slamming into the person with the knife, bowling them over. Two officers bolted after her, pulling her off the heirophant. The point of the knife blade caught Melinda's shoulder. Murmuring the St. Michael prayer, I started shooting film, aiming more for action than accuracy.

"You have interfered, constable. I would free this young man," the heirophant said in a sing-songy voice.

"You have the right to remain silent. Anything more you say can be used against you in a court of law," one of the officers replied, starting to handcuff the heirophant.

"I will enter no court but my king's," the heirophant said. By some inhuman strength, they twisted free of the officer's grip and rushed up the staircase to the landing. One moment, the actor stood poised on the landing. The next moment, perhaps in a flash of unseasonable lightning, everything flickered. The next moment, the actor lay sprawled on their back on the steps, their neck bent at an unnatural angle. Two officers rushed toward the figure, but stopped in their tracks as they reached the now plainly dead actor, staring down at it, then staring around them. The younger officer staggered away, back to the sodden ground, before falling in a faint. The other, older officer leaned over the edge of the steps, dry-heaving. I didn't blame them, especially not later when I developed my shots.

The police arrested the troupe on trespassing charges, but they were later released with strict warnings not to go near the forest, much less put on any more theatrics there, under penalty of jail time. They brought Melinda and Jared to the hospital to be checked out after that attack. I hated to be the officer who had to inform the family of that one actor.

They questioned me and later Melinda, but they had nothing to stick us with. I, of course, played the freedom of the press card. It still amazes me how local officials start backing down prior to cutting you loose when you do that.

I thought I had the story of the season, if not the year. Halsey stopped growling about how involved I'd gotten into all the twists and turns of this story. It certainly wouldn't constitute Pulitzer-worthy material, but it offered the kind of spooky-ooky stuff that sells good at this time of year.

Till I opened the paper that was supposed to carry the initial coverage on the legend of the staircase, and found it missing. I went to Halsey asking (probably demanding) an explanation, but the look on his face hinted at things to come.

"We had to pull the story," he said. "And we're not running that story about the hugger-mugger in the forest, at least not the way you wrote it. The Feds got hold of it, made me drop it. I told them it was a violation of the First Amendment as it applies to the press. But they told me this wasn't the first time they'd had to resort to this. Back in the 1920s, they'd had to resort to similar tactics, when another local paper tried to run a similar story."

"Involving the Cabot Mansion Staircase in the woods?" I asked.

"That and another bunch of amateur actors trying to put on that weird play you wrote about," Halsey said. "They've been trying to keep it under wraps all this time."

"Well, ain't that all Roswell-like," I said.

Halsey looked at me sideways. "That thought crossed my mind."

I resigned myself to never seeing the article in print. The Feds collected everything: the copy of the play that belonged to Philips Academy, the floppy discs containing my rough drafts, all the prints of my photos. Halsey signed a check for twice my usual fee, which helped my bank account, but not seeing those hard-won photos in print galled me to no end. What little news turned up in the papers didn't tell the whole story: they described the muddle in the forest as "a college prank gone wrong". College prank, my flat feet. I've seen college pranks and that wasn't someone filling the campus fountain with soap flakes.

If I'd tried arguing, Halsey would have had my head. I've learned over the years when to pick my fights with the old bear and when to back down, and the time had come to back the heck down.

None of this stops me from keeping, in a hiding-hole that only I know the location of, the negatives from that night. I'm of a mind to destroy them, though I hang onto them to thwart the Feds. Holding them up to the light, one can see, on top of the landing, a shape in the rain, a figure like a smear of yellow, something like a crown of antlers on its head, its face pale, eyes and nose and mouth like the holes in a mask.

Snapshots of the Mayor of Carcosa

My experiences with and memories of Joe Pulver come in snapshot-size moments. Conversations via comments on Facebook. Little moments in video chats that left an impression on this impressionable young writer who'd recently found the online Lovecraftian and Weird fiction community. And an encounter in eldritch Providence, Rhode Island.

I first met Joe via the *Lovecraft eZine* and their Sunday night video chats via Youtube, with its shifting circle of guests and regulars. I quickly grew fond of Joe for his "cool uncle" air, like that older fella who always comes to the family cookouts, cigarette in hand, always with a wise word or a clever quip or a thoughtful insight. One conversation about collections lead to Joe sharing some of his voodoo doll collection, including one plush version with built in holes for the bamboo skewer "pins". The vid feed switched to another guest before it skipped back to Joe, just in time to catch him cuddling the plush voodoo doll like a big kid with a teddy bear. One of the most weirdly cute or cutely weird sights I'd ever seen! I even said as much in the peanut gallery chatter on the LeZ's Facebook fan page. In that moment, I fell in love with this guy, not in a romantic way but like a niece getting to know the chill uncle in the family. His verve for the King in Yellow mythos of Robert W. Chambers lead me to seek out this collection of stories, and the air of sheer weirdness about them drew me in completely.

One of his wise quips on writing stuck with me and grew into something I'd share with other writing friends, a few words of wisdom on originality, delivered in his rich. drawling baritone voice: "Mediocre writers *borrow* things. Great writers *steal* things." I've told this to people I know who've wondered if their ideas have been "done to death" or their story looks too much like something written by another, better know writer, and that they needn't worry about their take on a notion or a trope, as long as they make the idea their own with their own slant on it. I'd eventually steal a few pages out of Chambers and write a few King in Yellow tales of my own, one of which later appeared alongside one of Joe's, in Atlantean Publishing and Carrion Blue's *A Terrible Thing*.

I finally met him in "carbonspace", in legend-haunted Providence, Rhode Island, at Necronomicon 2015, in the foyer of the Biltmore Hotel, just after an interview with Ramsay Campbell, one of that year's Guests of Honor. Appropriately, he and Katrin, his wife, was chatting with Ramsay and a few others from the Lovecraft eZine. I approached and introduced myself, how I was one of the peanut gallery commenters and how I'd recently started reading his *King in Yellow Tales* and utterly fell in love with his writing. "Awww, glad yah like 'em," he said and beckoned me into a hug which, as a natural hugger, I gladly gave him. Mike Davis and a few others including Ramsay Campbell were heading out for lunch. Joe invited me to join them and I gladly tagged along. I spent the next hour over Mexican food at a restaurant around the corner and down several doors on Washington Street, listening to these gentle giants of Weird fiction, like R. H. Barlow meeting a certain old Gentleman from Providence.

The next day, I bumped into Joe again, this time on the way up to an author reading for the release of Lois Gresh's *Innsmouth*

Nightmares. I'd gotten onto one of the elevators in the Biltmore, heading for one of the smaller ballrooms, and regulars at NecronomiCon's Providence iteration will tell you how unpredictably these conveyances can behave. A group of tall, husky young men got on, with Joe getting on last.

The elevator ascended for a few seconds, then juddered to a stop, apparently between floors. The young guys muttered in concerned German. Joe added, "That doesn't feel good." I playfully offered to climb up on someone's shoulders and peek out the hatch. Said Joe, "My back ain't so good, but maybe one of these guys 'll give you a boost." The young guys chuckled at this quip, and the elevator lurched back into motion. Later, following that reading, he'd sign my copy of *Innsmouth Nightmares*, a spur of the moment purchase which I treasure to this day, for the stories it contains and for the memories attached to it, of an unforgettable character and one of the warmest souls in Weird fiction.

I wish I could have had more moments with Joe; his passing in 2020 has hit me as hard as (and in some cases harder than) the loss of a family member. But he lives on via the archived video chats of the LeZ and more importantly, in his gritty yet wondrous tales. Sometimes, when I read them, my mind imagines Joe's voice, reading out loud, in a manner of speaking. Then the veil seems to lift and the Mayor of Carcosa looks out of the shadow, cigarette between his fingers, a friendly smirk under his long mustaches....

Don't miss out!

Visit the website below and you can sign up to receive emails whenever R.C. Mulhare publishes a new book. There's no charge and no obligation.

https://books2read.com/r/B-A-CWKI-CWWJB

BOOKS 2 READ

Connecting independent readers to independent writers.

About the Author

R.C. Mulhare was born in Lowell, Massachusetts and grew up in one of the surrounding towns, in a hundred year old house up the street from an old cemetery. Her interest in the dark and mysterious started when she was quite young, when her mother read the faery tales of the Brothers Grimm and quoted the poetry of Edgar Allan Poe to her, while her Irish storyteller father infused her with a fondness for strange characters and quirky situations. When she isn't writing, she moonlights in grocery retail. She's also fond of hiking in the woods of the White Mountains of New Hampshire, and browsing the antiques shops one finds all over New England. A two-time Amazon best-selling author, contributor to the Hugo nominated Archive of Our Own, and member of the New England Horror Writers, her work has also appeared with Atlantean Publishing, Macabre Maine, FunDead Publications. Nocturnal Sirens Publishing, Deadman's Tome, NEHW Press, DBND Publishing, and Weirdbook Magazine, with more stories releasing almost every month. She shares her home with her family, two small parrots, about fifteen hundred books and an unknown number of eldritch things that rattle in the walls when she's writing late in the night....

Read more at https://www.facebook.com/rcmulhare/.